HER 37TH YEAR

AN INDEX

HER 37TH YEAR

AN INDEX

SUZANNE SCANLON

NOEMI PRESS
LAS CRUCES NEW MEXICO

Cover Design: Evan Lavender-Smith
Interior Design: Steve Halle & Evan Lavender-Smith

LIBRARY OF CONGRESS CATALOGING-IN-PUBLICATION DATA

Scanlon, Suzanne.
  Her 37th year, an index / Suzanne Scanlon.
    pages ; cm
  ISBN 978-1-934819-42-5
  I. Title. II. Title: Her thirty-seventh year, an index.
  PS3619.C2665H47 2015
  813'.6—dc23
                            2015004673

Published by Noemi Press, Inc. a nonprofit literary
organization. www.noemipress.org

*Write books only if you are going to say in them the things
you would never dare confide to anyone.*
                                                —E. M. Cioran

*For some reason while I was peeing I thought about
Lawrence of Arabia.*
                        —David Markson (*Wittgenstein's Mistress*)

ANECDOTE, She tells him that she is writing a book about him. She asks if he's heard the one about Flannery O'Connor and the young and handsome textbook salesman. He took her for a drive, kissed her. She didn't know how to kiss. *I had a feeling of kissing a skeleton*, he wrote in a letter to a friend. Some weeks later, upon hearing that he'd married, she sat down to write "Good Country People"; she sent the finished story to him with a note: *This is not about you.*

BELIEF, In the height of summer, just past the solstice, she fell into what her doctors characterized as a chthonic depression. She'd been off medication too long; she lost weight; she wasn't sleeping—*sort of classic and boring,* she described it to a friend. She explained something of her desire to the young specialist: for sleep, for God, for travel, for transcendence; he responded, "I don't think you *really* feel that way. I think that's the *voice of depression* talking." She wants to believe the young doctor, to believe that her beliefs—her *overvalued* beliefs—are borne of a chemical disorder. Something separate from what she feels to be herself.

BEAUTY (see also: Morality, and Weakness), as when your teacher described a poet: "I was overwhelmed by how unattractive she was—not *just* overweight, but 6 feet tall—with carrot orange hair and tattoos. I thought, *This is too much, aggressive*—and then— " He paused, shook his head. "She began to read her poetry and—it was—beautiful. This was a lesson to me."

BODY, as when she walks in the city these days and her past walks beside her. Varick Street becomes 7th Ave South, where she passes a park district gym, now called "Recreation Center." On the treadmill, through the glass: a younger version of herself. In the locker room, an older woman—*my age now*, she considers— will comment on her naked body: "I used to have your body," the woman tells her. *I used to have my body*, she thinks.

BOREDOM (see also: Inner Resources, and Marriage), which Tolstoy defined as *the desire for desires*.

BOWLES, JANE (see also: Belief, Husband, Loss, and Need)

BREAKFAST (see also: Lack), during which, for example, your husband will read aloud from his computer screen: "Women between ages 35 and 45 are prone to sexual fury & fantasy—a desire for 'casual sex or flings or one night stands'—due to waning fertility." You will be eating cornmeal pancakes with clotted cream, raspberry jam. "It says here that this is a response, nature's way of compensating for that lack."

BUTLER, JUDITH (see also: Meaning): "If I cannot tell a story about myself, then I will die."

CABBAGES (see also: Happiness; and Woolf, Virginia): "Sally asked (she herself was extremely happy); for, she admitted, she knew nothing about them, only jumped to conclusions, as one does, for what can one know even of the people one lives with every day? She asked Are we not all prisoners? She had read a wonderful play about a man who scratched on the wall of his cell, and she had felt that was true of life—one scratched on the wall. Despairing of human relationships (people were so difficult), she often went into her garden and got from her flowers a peace which men and women never gave her. But no; he did not like cabbages; he preferred human beings, Peter said."

CAKE, which you eat as you sit in the cafe, waiting for him. "I'll be wearing a black jacket," he's told you, "and leather boots." Frances McDormand is sipping tea at the next table. You find it difficult not to stare. She stares back, in a nice way. She isn't wearing makeup. She is beautiful in real life, more beautiful than she appears on film, and this reminds you of something.

CHURCH (see also: Home), how a student speaks of faith: "I am a believer," she declares, explaining away a Larkin poem. Magoo, the Baby, obsesses over churches: St. Benedict, St. Ita, St. Gertrude. All Saints. The two of you visit churches; you, too, are still hungry for, as Larkin writes, *a serious house on serious earth*.

CIORAN, EMIL, of whom Sontag wrote: "His kind of writing is meant for readers who in a sense already know what he says."

CLOSURE, as when you tell him, the man who wears Timberland boots that remind you of your now-dead teacher, that it was his fault, that he took advantage, that you were vulnerable. Also: what you hoped his arrival might offer, what we all hope for: the knowledge that *one lover will call up a past love or experience*, the knowledge that *fantasy will intermingle with reality*.

COCOA (see also: Beckett, Samuel), In those days, I wanted only female profs. I wouldn't have known what to do with you in those days. I set limits; only later did I decide that the limits were too limiting. But that semester, there was the one non-negotiable male prof, and he was lovely. He taught late Ionesco and later Beckett and it had to do with *Godot* that a confident, overly handsome student challenged the wise, sad Prof, complaining: "Beckett's vision is so bleak. Yes, we're all sitting out here in a cold parking lot, waiting for a god who won't show up, but why can't we share some cocoa, warm each other up while we're out here?"

COLUMBIA (see also: Emptiness, Light, and Memory), as when she writes to him,

> Dearest, It is almost four on a Friday afternoon and I am walking across the old campus in Morningside Heights. As I pass Butler Library, the light shifts and I become aware of the sensation which I link to the grandeur of a school I was once privileged enough to call home, to walk in a late December afternoon sun thinking only of the nothingness around me, un-held in that specific darkness. That enormous lack, the memory of how it could not be sated. The awareness of a hospital, which became home uptown—the lingering fear they would send me there, where I would never

get out because it would not be possible to walk again in the waning light of afternoon. To walk in Riverside Park, on Morningside Drive. The street carries the smell of a hospital gown, a sharps container, my clothes in a plastic bag. I am Travis Bickle who are you? Yes, my love—that is what I meant to ask: who are you?

COMMUNICATION (see also: Art, Life, Love, and You), as when she quotes Tony Kushner: *"The individual is a myth. The lowest reducible unit of humanity is two."* The essence of humanity is the pair: Didi and Gogo, Hamm and Clov, Pozzo and Lucky. Or the way she ends a letter: *Even if you don't, or won't—I write because I can imagine you, there, reading. I don't exist without you.*

CONFESSION (see also: Language), as when the man in boots wants to talk: "There are so many things about myself that I want to tell you." You want to stay on the phone for hours. You will fall in love with his voice, which is not the body, but is a link to it.

CONSEQUENCES, It may cause you to suffer: the wetness of your panties, your desire to be touched by a married man.

CONTAINMENT (see also: Memory, and Theater),

Dearest, I was watching a woman on stage last night, a young woman, and I had a memory of a woman from the ward. Meredith. There, she was something of an aberration. Everything about her was contained. She was perpetually tan, and somehow maintained a crisp short blond haircut. She wore tennis skirts and tight little sundresses that revealed her thick tan legs, punctuated by white Keds. She smoked Virginia Slims. She was from Greenwich, she would be sure to tell you. She would talk with the Aides and laugh but when she laughed her mouth only opened so far and the rest of her face didn't move. There was such a sadness about her—the containment—so it didn't bother me or anyone too much the way she looked down on the others: Ava with her scars, Maria with her fingers down her throat, Jennifer with her various personalities. Jennifer who, we all knew, would never leave. Jennifer who had become a part of the place. Jennifer whose father raped her face down in his work shed. Jennifer who still ate nails, liked the taste of nails, couldn't help herself.

COURTSHIP, as when he asks for more. *I want to read you,* he will write.

CUPCAKE, as when you walk together to the counter, your arm brushing against his jacket sleeve. He will say,

"Let me handle this," which you like. You eat chocolate cupcakes with chocolate frosting and yellow sugar flowers. Your body will feel like it's on fire. You will want so badly to be touched by this man in boots. Afterward you will call a friend, who will refer you to his expensive healer. You will call the expensive healer. She will call you "sweetie." She will tell you that it's going to be okay. To want to be touched is not the worst thing, she will advise.

DAVIS, STUART (see also: Diary, Manifesto, and The Morgan Library): "There are two things in the world—life and death. 'Art' is life. 'Not art' is death."

DEATH (see also: Friendship),

Dearest, Last night I went out for expensive Korean food with a girlfriend. I drank one glass of wine and felt a little drunk. She is so intense, my friend. Later I had that Kierkegaardian feeling: that I give her too much, that she takes something of me, from me, that it's vampiric, our friendship. She tells me her mother had this intensity. I don't know what it would be like to have a mother so invested in my well-being, I don't know and so I take this from my friend, vampiric; this is why I love her, why I was first drawn to her. She cares about me and she tells me this. I care about you, she says. I believe her. Is that foolish? Later while driving home we decided that we're each having a midlife crisis, in our own personal special stupid ways. Her childhood friend has cancer, she explained: "And I feel like saying to her, *Now really did you have to get cancer? Do you have to remind me that we're all going to die, that I'm also going to die, which is something I cannot accept right now? At all. Really did you have to?*" She started to cry. "I get it," I said. We laughed then. "I care about you, too," I said. I never say things like this to friends, but she brings it out in me. She makes me a better friend. Which is why I will say it here to you, too, my dearest: I care about you.

DESIRE (see also: DuBois, Blanche; Boredom; and Creation), a friend describes this way: "My crushes are usually like, *I want him to fuck me against the wall right now.*" Another friend explains: "I see affairs everywhere. Marriage—monogamy, rather—means that I will never reach my sexual potential."

DESPAIR (see also: Asylum, and Teaching),

Dearest, And yet: these moments of extreme existential despair! As in: here are all of these minds/selves in the room with me and not one seems to give a whit what I'm going on about. Or that whole thing where I am the only person in the room with any energy/interest/ enthusiasm at all for the subject. Even when I'm faking it, I'm the only one faking it. At times, the room functions as a microcosm of the world-at-large, reminding me again of why I have long desired only to remove myself from the world-at-large.[1] I think I'd prefer to spend the rest of my life in a mental hospital; that is, if it wasn't really a mental hospital, but instead was some sort of utopian alterna-space, a true asylum. Can you and I create this space? I think we've begun.

DESK (see also: Acker, Kathy), on which you've pasted words from a book that once broke you open: "Writing is one method of dealing with being human or wanting to suicide cause in order to write you kill yourself at the same time while remaining alive."

DEVORAH, from an Orthodox family, you meet in group therapy. Once her therapist had told her to masturbate. She never had. "And so he said, *I will show you how.*" He began to show her— "*like* this,' he said, hands

---

[1] When asked, "What is the role of the artist in society?" Jean-Philippe Toussant replied, "To run away."

moving near to his thighs"—but she left[2] the office, never to return.

DISAPPOINTMENT (see also: Hateful Things; and Shonagon, Sei), as when the man in boots dresses hurriedly, late for his next appointment. As when he cannot find his jacket, scarf. Keys. As when she pulls a crisp sheet over her bare breast, tries to remember the words of Sei Shonagon, who wrote of lovers in her pillow book.[3] After all, I too learned long ago that *the end is contained within the beginning*, but still, you needn't have mentioned it right there in bed, so soon after the fucking.

DISCOURSE (see also: Desire, Love, (M)essay, Revolution, and You), I don't want to write a mommy narrative or a menopause narrative. As Eileen Myles said, *I want to… [be] punk about aging*. I won't fit into what is allowed.

---

[2] which is what I will come to think sometimes—that I should have left, too, but I was not so strong. I was always too curious, too eager to see what would happen next.

[3] "Indeed, one's attachment to a man depends largely on the elegance of his leave-taking. When he jumps out of bed, scurries about the room, tightly fastens his trouser-sash, rolls up the sleeves of his Court cloak, over-robe, or hunting costume, stuffs his belongings into the breast of his robe and then briskly secures the outer sash—one really begins to hate him."

I want to be messy, to be here. Where I am, which is a mess, feels honest. A friend says, "You're *a hot mess.*" I won't create that archetype. I want to deny the arch. I don't want to become a power woman, masculinized, my hair *done*. What they've created: *nymphet cougar mother-in-law dame.* No. I want to be punk about aging, punk about gooey mothering, punk about turning thirty-eight, thirty-nine, forty.

DISORIENTATION, as when she tells him she needs a break. He is too much. She's become attached and it's fucking her up. As when she asks, "Don't you see how it is all about the impossible trajectory of hope?" Or when he answers, "Yes, I do." "I admire you," he says, with sadness.

DISTURBED, THE (see also: Body, Comfort, Elegy, and Whitney Museum of American Art), as when you recall your teacher[4] quoting *his* teacher "who used to say that the job of fiction, of good art, is to *comfort the disturbed*, and *disturb the comfortable*." (Or when a man pulls his wife away from Paul Thek's *Meat Pieces*, whispering: *This is human flesh!*) I tell a mutual friend that I find the

---

[4] who also wore boots.

linking of our teacher's persona to his oft-quoted commencement address problematic. (It has, after all, been adapted into an "uplifting" viral video.) The speech contained good advice, but it was not exactly advice our teacher lived out in a day-to-day way. He could be kind and loving;[5] he was often capable of hideous cruelty. In this regard, his mourners' naive reverence can feel pathetic. What we mourn is the *idea* of our teacher, the one presented in the speech to the graduates. The one who knew what it meant to be a good person, even if he was not able to be that person. For most of us, this is as good as it gets. Aspiration. Recognition. Searching, striving for that impossible thing. To fail regularly.[6]

---

[5] Desire was the way he and I kissed each other as if looking for something else, not the other, and it made us both sad. But we were already sad. That was desire. Desire was the way he liked that there was a man in my house if not my bed and he liked that I left that man in sweatpants at his house one day and desire was him feeding the man's pants to his dog. Desire was the way he took me to the grocery store in his new car and desire was him telling me "you're hot" and me thinking, *oh is he just like all the rest* because he did say *hot* he called me *hot*—him even him. Especially him.

[6] A friend will not allow that madness is beyond rational argument. He will not allow that within his moralizing assessment of boredom (*How dare we be bored!*) he has aligned himself with Henry's mother

DREAMS, of airplanes, tall buildings, healing; you wake at 2 a.m. to see the Manhattan skyline over the promenade. You know yourself again, or think you do. *I am home. I am home,* you say to the sky, the water, the possibility of all things.

DRESS, as when the bride, with her complete aura of integrity, wore red. How much sense it made. How I loved the dress I wore on my own wedding day but how it was completely wrong. How I lack integrity; my aura is that of someone playing dress-up.

DRUGS, as when you might imagine another way to live.

DURAS, MARGUERITE (see also: DuBois, Blanche): "Grief is the most important thing in my life."

DUBOIS, BLANCHE (see also: Desire; Duras, Marguerite, and Grief), Still the city, on occasion, could be this way: all kindness, all strangers.

---

in Berryman's poem; he has declared our teacher lacking inner resources and he has blamed our teacher, our friend, for that lack.

EMAIL, You will read his, only one line—*looking forward to hearing your voice*—and it will make you wet. The man in boots eschews capitalization, which somehow makes the note sexier. If it were from a student, you would not find the use of lowercase sexy; you would find it disrespectful, an indication of stupidity. You sit at your desk wet, wondering at the link between language and desire. You walk into the classroom. You teach the poems of Edna St. Vincent Millay with your panties wet. You wonder if this is the only real thing in the world anymore, the only true thing: the wetness of your panties.

EMPTINESS (see also: Nelson, Maggie; and Weil, Simone), of which Nelson writes, "For some, the emptiness itself is

God; for others, the space must stay empty." Your Israeli doctor notes that you are *starving at a banquet*. These nights, the theater, that city. An impossible banquet, but nonetheless: "I was fed. I did not starve!" you declare in retrospect. "This was your nostalgia, perhaps, but for me, for some of us: the emptiness itself is God." When all falls away, you call it Post-Play Depression; and someday this, too, will be in the DSM. Pathologize the ending; pathologize loss; pathologize the condition of being alive. The doctor tells you that it was all, of course, merely symbolic. Symbolic of what? Of life, of loss, "which you haven't yet found your way around." "Have you, doctor?" "Have I what?" "Have you found your way?"

ENCARNACION BAIL ROMERO (see also: Horror, and Mothers) is a woman variously described as an *undocumented,* a *migrant worker,* an *illegal immigrant*. The Kansas poultry processing plant where Romero works is raided and her two-year old baby, Carlos, is taken from her. She is put in jail. Carlos is detained by the State until adopted by a family who renames him Jamison.

END, THE (see also: Healing), "You are not finished," she assures you. It would be easier to be finished, you often think. You have thought.

ENDGAME (see also: Beckett, Samuel; Life; and Theater), as when the man steps out to find a toilet, and she listens to the women seated behind her, waiting for the play to begin.[1]

ERNAUX, ANNIE (see also: Death, Love, and Writing), who

---

[1] "He's trying to set me up with his brother. But his brother is older than he is!"

"What is he, 104?"

"I guess. I don't need that. I don't need to take care of someone."

"No, you don't. You need someone younger than you."

"Yes. I need a companion."

"Yes.

"It's the loneliness. The loneliness is awful."

"Yes."

"And it doesn't get better."

"No."

"It doesn't get better. Listen, I'll tell you—the loneliness is the shits. It's the shits!"

"And there's nothing to be done about it."

"No. As my friend Ronnie says, It is what it is."

"It is what it is."

"Some things you can't change."

"No, some things we can't change. We change the things we can change. The rest, we try to accept."

"Sometimes we change the things we can change."

"We don't always."

"No."

"My daughter tells me, Go on JDate. JDate!"

writes: "Whether or not he was 'worth it' is of no consequence. And the fact that all this is gradually slipping away from me, as if it concerned another woman, does not change this one truth: thanks to him, I was able to approach the frontier separating me from others, to the extent of actually believing that I could sometimes cross over it."

ESTHER (see also: Ghosts), who was 30 when we met. She'd gone to my same college and, for this reason, liked me. Her face was shaped by a smile, with the glossy-eyed gaze of a madwoman. Her husband had once visited, remarked on her luck: weren't we all having such a lovely time, taking this break and wouldn't

---

"I don't want to do that."

"No."

"You don't want a lover."

"No."

"I'm not looking for a lover. I'm looking for someone to tell me 'you should do this. You shouldn't do that.'"

"Right."

"My friend Audrey—she found someone on JDate. A young guy. She's rich, of course."

"Right. I don't need that."

"No."

"It is what it is."

"It sure is."

he like a break? *But, gee.* Someone had to pay the bills. Someone had to take care of the kids. His bitterness. She had two young children, a boy and a girl, who had to wait in the lobby. Later when the doctors decided to send me to the Long-Term Ward, Esther confided that she was jealous, that she wanted to go to the *famous* ward, but it was too late. She'd aged, had a family. Time is on your side,[2] she whispered into my ear that last day, before being discharged to her mother's home in Babylon.

EXCEPTIONS, as when your husband declares that he loves you but feels three things: bored, lonely, and invisible. Also: he thought this sort of longing, desperation, was only for sad old people.

EXHILARATION, as how within a certain inspired state, every tiny thing becomes of consequence. How exhausting. *Exhilarated despair.* A desire for obliteration.

---

[2] Which was a cliché whose tragic import I would only and necessarily understand years later, with much less of it beside me.

FAILURE (see also: Body), A student reads Joe Brainard, her face flushed as she reads aloud of the day he went home to paint with his dick. *I would like for once to know what it is to have a dick.* The idea morphs into a discourse on the body—that we must write from the body, that the body is linked to writing, to words. Next, another student tells us she almost killed her younger brother as a child. *It was an accident.* Her mother saved his life. "It is so easy to fail!" I exclaim, nearing hysteria. We edge toward her as she reads. I link Joe Brainard's dick to our visceral response, to the way we gasped as we felt the plight of the small boy, a jawbreaker lodged in his fragile throat.

FAREWELL (see also: Relief; Rendezvous; and Shonagon, Sei),

"This is going to be awkward,"[1] the man in boots announces, before saying good-bye. *To declare something awkward does not foreclose responsibility for the moment itself*, you write.

FANTASY, A dog will present as a lobster, a child as a serpent. A young girl writes on her Tumblr: *Wait so like there are other people out there having fantasies about checking into the psych ward? #everythingissowhite #plustheyfeedyouchemicals*

FEMINAISSANCE (see also: Kraus, Chris; and *Écriture feminine*), in which Kraus writes: "There is always too much feeling in female writing, but feeling itself isn't the point. It is intellectual vaudeville. It arrives at the moment of feeling, then leaves. It demonstrates something: itself."

FETISH (see also: Love), when Elizabeth Hardwick moved to New York she wrote to her mother: *Dear Mama: I love Columbia. Of course I do. The best people here are all Jews—what you call "Hebrews."* Her goal, Hardwick often said, was "to become a New York Jewish intellectual."

---

[1] Not the word I would have used.

FIREWORKS, as when I loved B—, as when he wouldn't love me enough, as when we went to see the Macy's fireworks display. This was the only time during those years that I celebrated the Fourth of July. I had been otherwise too unhappy to do American things. But that day, looking up to those fireworks, I thought to myself: *I am happy. This is happiness.*[2] Or: *If this is happiness, I'll take it*, a girl thinks, me. On our way to the East Side to see the fireworks, we'd stopped at a bodega; we ate cherries and dried mangoes. I was wearing a black dress.[3]

---

[2] There is a moment in *The Hours*, the film version of Michael Cunningham's book, a film which, I'd argue, transcends the novel itself, not least of all by the inclusion of Meryl Streep as a present-day Clarissa Dalloway, now living with a woman (Allison Janney) in Manhattan. There is a moment where Streep is in bed, recalling the past, telling her daughter: "I remember thinking, this was the beginning of happiness. But no, that was it. That wasn't the beginning. That was happiness."

[3] There is more I want to say about that black dress. It was thin sheer cotton, breezy and long and I wore it in the winter with a leotard underneath, with tights and a sweater. In the summer I wore it with very little underneath, a black bra and underwear. I wore it to Lincoln Center to see an Amy Sedaris play. I wore it to audition for graduate school theater programs, including the one I turned down because I couldn't bear the thought of leaving New York. Of leaving a certain person.

FLU SHOT (see also: Conflict, and Marriage), "I'm getting my flu shot." "Okay." "Do you want to come with me?" "No." "When will you get yours?" Though there are at least 18 things you'd prioritize over getting your flu shot, marriage makes manifest this pressure. A pressure which you don't want to feel, given that you have all variety of personal, internal pressures. If you ignore this external pressure you are risking further conflict in your marriage: that large thing that has become so much more than the two of you.

FORTY (see also: Death, Milestones, and Montaigne), and suddenly every book is about turning that age: Chris Kraus: "As I turn forty, can I avenge the ghost of my former self?" Forty as the end *and* the beginning: Carole Maso's *Ava*, Martin Amis' *The Information*, David Foster Wallace's "My Appearance" or "Good Old Neon." Claudia Rankine: "It occurs to me that forty could be half my life or it could be all my life. On the television I am told that I don't want to look like I am forty. Forty means I might have seen something hard, something unpleasant, or something dead. I might have seen it and lived beyond it in time." A friend explains: "For me it led to a certain crisis point. I became convinced that I had to sleep with someone who was not my husband. It was the first time I saw desire so clearly, as an antidote to death, to mortality." "Did it work?" "Not really."

FRAGILITY, as when the man in boots says, "I think we should do this until we don't want to anymore. And then we will go back to being friends." Now, she wonders when that will be. She knows that it all rests *just so*, but the end should not be named. She wants to tell him. The transience, its effervescence, is much of the charm. Later, her husband will speak of power-grabs and possession. Later still, she will tell the man it is over. "Why?" "It has long been my tendency to push toward conclusion."

FREEDOM (see also: Aging, and Death), You drink wine with a friend and speak of the real shit of it. "It's weird aging, right? It's like, 'What the fuck is that?'" you say, misquoting the movie *Greenberg*, in which Baumbach's Ben Stiller has been disfigured into a regular person, a mentally ill loser, even. The sentiment lacks eloquence, yet is true. How irrelevant we must seem![4] "I know this is horrible," your friend confesses, "but I feel ashamed

---

[4] Or, as Dodie Bellamy writes in *The Buddhist*: "Middle aged women are such an easy target."

of getting older." "I get it," you say. "It's like that Nora Ephron book: I read the title now and think, *I get it*. I never wanted to get it, Nora Ephron!" To the man in boots, you say: "I was so young once!" It's your favorite line from *Hiroshima, Mon Amour*—when the French actress says so to her Japanese lover, to the universe. Privately you wonder if your writing has been just this, a histrionic assertion: *I was young once!*

FRIENDSHIP (see also: Love, Desire, and Death), as when you discover there isn't language for this sort of friendship, for what the man in boots is to you.

FUCKING (see also: Writing),—and sometimes I want to write about fucking but mostly I want to write about love. This is why I write or have ever written. As if trying to love. His soon-to-be ex-wife told B—, the man I loved in those days, that she had never loved him. She told him this some years into the marriage. When he wanted children, which she didn't want. Plus she stopped sleeping with him. But what really destroyed him was the declaration that she'd never loved him. His suffering kept him from loving me as much as I needed to be loved, but also made me more deeply in love, such that I believed that could I feel how he suffered.

GAZE, THE (see also: *Good Morning Midnight,* and Rhys, Jean): In the novel Sasha walks home, tells herself that she is "not at all sad"; she is tired, merely. *Just then two men come up from behind and walk along on either side of me. One of them says: 'Pourquoi etes-vous si triste?'* Sasha decides "Yes, I am sad"—then it's been decided, her subjective experience altered through this vision of herself under the gaze, her self an unsmiling, tired object. In my New York (of the nineties) I walked freely, broke, sad, tired. Now if you have a certain openness, a vulnerability—a man will ask: "Why so sad?" Or, lost in thought, you will hear a voice behind you: "Smile!"

GHOSTS (see also: Ground Zero, Holiday, and Hotel): a loneliness I wanted to explain to my husband but could not. The thwarted urge itself as revelatory. We wake to bulldozers resisting absence, recreating upon the site of death; I wonder at the difference between destruction and construction. The thought that I might try to explain; and if I did try, that he would listen and not be angry or distant. This is enough. When the sounds are all the same, when the air is full of dust, when you feel your fate distilled to heroes, tourists, cameras.

GINSBERG, ALLEN, who spoke of self-rejection, how you internalize all you've been told is wrong with you; how you bring that out into the world with you. What it was for him to leave a psych ward; how he walked the streets of the city seeking validation[1] everywhere, finding it nowhere. *I am with you in Rockland, Q—!* How he knew then he had to leave New York.

GOOD PEOPLE (see also: Tragedy),

My dearest, You are a good person and because you are a good person I am going to like you even more than I

---

[1] What I mean is that it was time to move on, and moving on meant acquiring a real-world, non-mental patient boyfriend. This boyfriend would turn out to break my heart. For all of the reasons that he would love me, he couldn't love me. I would internalize this limitation and extrapolate it to a rejection of me, a referendum on my ability to be successful as an integrated human being.

already do. But still there might exist a part of me that wishes you were not such a good person, that instead you would say let's meet somewhere for a day or a night. And if you said that I would say yes. And we would meet, and have really hot sex, and it would be great. Afterward, we would return to our conventional lives where we attempt to be good people. But instead, of course, you say, "Let's be friends!" and I say, "Yes, let's!" And we become friends in the manner of Oscar Wilde, where friendship is more tragic than love, if only because it lasts longer.

GOODBYE, when years ago you left this city in order to leave B—, (or so you told yourself), who was married and going through a divorce. You loved B— but couldn't imagine being with him for ten more years, or even five. Still, you couldn't leave *him*; you weren't capable. Instead, you had to leave New York City; only consequently would you leave B—.[2]

---

[2] It is better to be the one who leaves, even if you are leaving a place like New York. It was only years later that I realized I had indeed left the city of my own volition. The realization surprised me. At the time I was so relieved to be leaving him—if accidentally on-purpose—that I neglected to consider the fact of leaving the city itself. At times, this felt like a mistake.

HABIT (see also: "One Art," and Loss), which is what you will tell yourself it was, what B— was, and that's all, easy enough to (*Write it!*) disavow.

HANDOUT, as when the doctor presents a form titled: CONTAINMENT. It is not very unlike teaching, all the handouts. It is up to the student to read the handout. You read: *Learn to stay in control even when angry. Take time-outs. Challenge the myth that ventilating anger is healthy.* With red ink, you strike through the word ventilating. "What does it mean to be sick?" a student asks. "Is it to be always, forever, outside of it all?"

HAMLET (see also: Baby, The), We watch three film versions of *Hamlet.* I cry even when it is Bill Murray playing Polonious. I imagine my baby as Laertes. "Do you know how it is when someone dies? Birth is like that, too, just in reverse," I say. Just before you announce the impending awkwardness, I ask aloud, "How could I have created something, someone, whom I will some-day lose?" I think, *How could life mean anything more, ever, ever again?*

HAPPINESS (see also: Fireworks), which the monk defined as an ability to work with all that comes. Or what someone else described as the moment before you need more happiness.

HARDWICK, ELIZABETH (see also: Betrayal, and Hunger), "Se-duction may be baneful, even tragic, but the seducer at his work is essentially comic. The seducer as a type, or as an archetype, hardly touches upon any of our deep feelings unless there is some exaggeration in him, something complicated and tangled and mysterious-ly compelling about a nature that has come to define itself through the mere fact of sex. For the most part the word seduction; indicates effort of a persevering, thoughtful sort. A seduction is the very opposite of the abrupt, which is, of course, rape. The most interesting seducers are actually rapists; for instance, Don Giovan-ni and Lovelace. Their whole character is trapped in the moil of domination and they drudge on, never satisfied, never resting, mythically hungry."

HECTOR (see also: Jensen. Sasha; and *Good Morning, Midnight*), "He says: 'For me, you see, I look at life like this: If someone had come to me and asked me if I wished to be born I think I should have answered No. I'm sure I should have answered No. But no one asked me.'"

HEROINE (see also: Hardwick, Elizabeth), "She may, of course, begin with the hope, and romance would scarcely be possible otherwise; however, the truth hits her sharply, like vision or revelation when the time comes. Affections are not things and persons never can become possessions, matters of ownership. The desolate soul knows this immediately, and only the trivial pretend that it can be otherwise. When love goes wrong the survival of the spirit appears to stand upon endurance, independence, tolerance, solitary grief. These are tremendously moving qualities, and when they are called upon it is usual for the heroine to overshadow the man who is the origin of her torment."

HOLIDAY, when I took a hot bath. I spoke to you. I drank two glasses of wine. I kissed Magoo. I left the room. I had trouble communicating. I read three poems by three men. I read *The Pornographic Imagination*. I sleep. I dream of you.

HOMEOSTATIC, as in a conversation with my husband: "I had this empty feeling tonight." "Mmhmm," he said. He turned the pages of his book. *Sacred Cow* by Diamela Eltit. "And I realized that this emptiness is tied to the feeling of longing. That I am so used to longing as a way to fill that void. You know?" "Yes," he said, still looking at his book. "And what I realized was that I will always long for something. You see, once I longed to be married. It was what I wanted. Now I have it. But I still have that emptiness." "Right." "And it is not that the emptiness is the same. It is relieved by your company, by the fact of being loved—" "But it is still there." "It is a verb." "It is always there." "..." "What do you mean a verb?" "That that is how it must be. To satisfy it destroys it. So it moves elsewhere." "Yes." "Desire is a homeostatic system." "..." "Push it down in one place it rises in another." And then I told him about the woman in my class who writes these very sexy stories about her affairs with married men. "It really bothers some of the other students," I told him. "Too bad." "But I love it," I said. "..." "You can have an affair if you want."

"That's not what I'm saying." "It's okay." "Do you want to have an affair?" "Don't deflect." "You deflected first." "I was talking about my student." "Okay."

HOMEWORK: on a student essay, you write: *DO NOT CONFLATE NARRATOR W/ AUTHOR.* Another student begins an essay with this line: *Life is meaningful because it does not go on forever, and while we are living love is the most meaningful thing in our entire life's.*

HORROR (see also: Texas), as when the *New York Times* covers the story of an eleven year old girl gang-raped by fourteen men, quoting neighbors who say of the girl: "*[S]he dressed older than her age, wearing makeup and fashions more appropriate to a woman in her 20s. She would hang out with teenage boys at a playground,*" and "*Where was her mother? What was her mother thinking?*"

HOTEL (see also: Ghosts, and Love), where she works, teaching English to undocumented workers. Women who leave babies at home, work long hours and make nothing. Women who clean up the shit of rich people. This pathos. Sites of inequity. She leaves a big tip. The hotel sits near Ground Zero, near condos populated by young attractive women who carry yoga mats with their handbags. Despite this, the streets still reek of death. Signs for memorials, for Freedom Tower. Lists of heroes. Tourists with large cameras.

HUSBAND, who will call. "I miss you," you will say. "I love you," you will say. "I want to move back to New York," you will say. He will either not hear you or he will ignore you. "I have to get some work done," he will say. "We can talk tomorrow," he will say. "Goodnight. Love you." "Goodnight."

INFINITE JEST, in which the rather unsympathetic mother figure, Avril Incandenza, explains to her son: "There are, apparently, persons who are deeply afraid of their emotions, particularly the painful ones. Grief, regret, sadness. Sadness especially, perhaps. Dolores describes these persons as afraid of obliteration, emotional engulfment. As if something truly and thoroughly felt would have not end or bottom. Would become infinite and engulf them."

IONESCO, EUGENE, as when the man in boots takes you to a terrible production of *The Chairs*. Later in bed, you recite a scene from *Man With Bags*. An old woman in the wheelchair meets her young mother, who appears the way she remembered her frozen in time, the way early death does this; they meet now in an after-death place.

OLD WOMAN: Mommy? Mommy! Here!

YOUNG WOMAN: There you are, baby. Oh, darling...

OLD WOMAN: Oh, mommy, I thought you were gone! I'm so happy to see you! So happy! I gave up. I think about you all the time. I forget you're gone and then when I remember...oh mommy!...it breaks my heart!

YOUNG WOMAN: Look at you darling, my baby, your eyes haven't changed a bit. They're exactly the way they used to be when you played with dolls. I remember...

OLD WOMAN (*hugging YOUNG WOMAN tightly*): I was so happy when we were together. After you left, mama, there was such a difference...such an empty feeling...I could never shake it. You can't believe the things that've happened to me!

IRELAND, or, you meet a man from County Clare. "You are a Siobhan," he will tell you, which was what your mother wanted to name you before her friends advised otherwise. "Are you Irish?" Red-faced wasted Irishman.

"I am," he answers, all sexy brogue. "I am too," you say, Midwest valley girl. "I can see that," he says. He wants to tell you—he wants to tell you that "what you did up there"—you read—"very brave and honest and groundbreaking"—he wants to tell you that "there will be a backlash there will be retribution there *must be* for such honesty." He wants to tell you that "tomorrow you may wake up with a headache here and here"—he will touch the softness of your face. He will touch your temples and say "I want you to do this"—he will refer to your chakras. "You are an open soul," he will say, and you take your shoes off as you nod; you listen as if he is an oracle.

JANUARY (see also: Exclusivity, Memory, and Teacher), one of cream-colored corduroy pants, a powder blue V-neck sweater. We talked about a Daphne Merkin essay in that week's *New Yorker* in which she wrote about being in the hospital where I've been. A New York hospital. "I've eaten tapioca pudding on the fifth floor, too," our teacher confided, an exquisite intimacy. Later he would say of his colleague: "You read and have the sense that *she shouldn't be doing this.*" The implication is that *this*— this writing—is what *I* should be doing. This glorious, wretched club, which might have me as a member.

JENNIFER (see also: Auden), The other thing about the man who wouldn't love me: he said that the problem with his wife and their sex life had to do with her incest history. That she could never have a normal sex life. I thought of Jennifer from the ward. It was this way for her too. Sex was always submission, victimization. Jennifer made jewelry, sitting at a table in the back of the ward's dining room. She was never allowed out but would send others with money to buy beads, stones of clay and glass, resins and metals, plastics and chains.

JENSEN, SASHA (see also: *Good Morning Midnight*): "If I must end like one or the other, may I end like the hag."

JEWISH (see also: Baby, The; and Mother): "Let's talk about death now," Magoo suggests cheerfully; I pick decals off a tin thermos. "Let's talk about what happens when we die!" Later, before bed: "Maria isn't Jewish. Amy either. Leah is Jewish. Am I Jewish?" "Yes, I say." "Are you Catholic?" He asks. "Sort of," I say. "Well I grew up that way. I went to church and catholic school. I prayed and did the sacraments. But I don't anymore." "Oh." "I still pray sometimes." "When?" "When I'm in an airplane. Or when you were in my belly." "Yeah. I remember that." "What?" "When I was in your tummy." "You do? "It was nice." "Huh." "A little squishy."

JOY (see also: Mother, Question, and Skunks), as experienced

when in a dark room I lie next to Magoo and his cous-
in. Every so often, just when I think they might be
asleep, a high voice with a serious question: "Are there
skunks in Pittsburgh?" or "Do old-fashioned cars go
faster than convertibles?" Four-year old musing & in-
quiry; for a moment, I wish that Magoo would be four
years old forever, that I might spend a life in this room
with two four year old boys. There are times it feels like
Heaven, to have this life.

KING STREET (see also: Advice, and Therapy), where you pass the office of a therapist you saw exactly once. A skills-trained therapist, back before DBT was hip: a woman who could only see you for a 6 a.m. appointment, in the middle of a life where you saw no one at 6 a.m. A woman who, as you moaned or complained or expressed a bit of post-adolescent despair, asked, "Have you read Cindy Crawford's new book?" Despite the horror & shock on your face, she quoted Cindy Crawford to you—a patient sitting in her carefully lit ground floor office—"Never let a pimple ruin your day!"

KRAUS, CHRIS (see also: *Feminaissance, I Love Dick*): "I think that 'privacy' is to contemporary female art what 'obscenity' was to male art and literature of the 1960s.

The willingness of someone to use her life as primary material is still deeply disturbing, and even more so if she views her own experience at some remove. There is no problem with female confession providing it is made within a repentant therapeutic narrative. But to examine things cooly, to thrust experience out of one's own brain and put it on the table, is still too confrontational."

LACK (see also: Phaedra; and Lacan, Jacques[1]), for when it began, B— did not love me enough. This is how it felt to me. That he would not love me enough and perhaps that was where it was meant to remain—with me wanting more, and him, just out of reach.

LEEK SOUP (see also: Duras, Marguerite; and Suicide)

LESSONS (see also: Habit, and "One Art"), as when you teach "One Art." You will tell your students that writing is like losing. That writing is losing. You correct yourself. They look confused. You try to explain. A student sits with his ass hanging out of his pants. You want to pull up his pants, contain him.

---

[1] who said, "Love is giving something you haven't got to someone who doesn't exist."

LIMINAL (see also: Life): "New York has become something between memory & fantasy," she tells the man in boots, who was born here and not there. She wants him to know something of the beautiful May day of her graduation: Madeline Albright's voice, her parents, an older brother and sister. A fear of endings. A failure of the imagination. Aloud to the man, she imagines Magoo's graduation—that she will be here, again, another beautiful May day. "Beware," the man will advise; "Your son will imagine his own future."

LISPECTOR, CLARICE (see also: Love, and Solitude): "At this time of day she often wishes to be alone and dead to everything in the world, except for the one man whom she does not yet know and whom she will create for herself."

LONELINESS (see also: Regret, and Maternity), You remember reading an interview with Anne Carson who said that loneliness is not a significant problem. The doctor will ask you, "How bad does it get, the loneliness?" You feel uncomfortable measuring such a thing; she's failed to understand your experience. She means to be comforting but the question only makes you lonelier.

LONGING (see also: Questions), I hate longing but I must not really because I am so good at it. You may feel connected to a former loneliness, an old friend.

LOVE (see also: Lispector, Clarice; and Madness): "So, she who knows that everything will end takes the man's free hand, and taking it in hers sweetly burns, burns, burns, and blazes."

MEDICAL BRACELET (see also: M.A.O.I.), "You should wear one, too," your teacher advised, "if you ever pass out somewhere and they want to give you an anesthetic." "I'm afraid." "Nardil interacts with anesthesia." he explained, then asked: "Afraid of what? A hypertensive crisis?" "To be marked."

M.A.O.I. The specialist noted it was saved for worst-case scenarios. Intractable cases. You feel stupidly special. You have been on and off every Selective-Serotonin-Reuptake-Inhibitor to no effect. You read somewhere that it "takes two" to be ill: patient and doctor.

MADNESS (see also: Love, Sontag, and Truth), as when Susan Sontag writes of Simone Weil and madness. We look to Weil for an undeniable truth, she allows. Within Weil's abdication, there is something vital—a madness with validity—and, though Sontag would not choose that truth, though no one would choose such a life for her child, we do recognize it as Truth; we need Weil's voice.

MAGOO (see also: Baby, The; Joy; and Life), You ask what is left: *Do I write about his little mouth that forms a tiny O? Do I write about his mewling or the mark on his left cheek, left from the day he cut himself too deeply with a nail I failed to trim? Should I write about naps, the nights that he sleeps so deeply like last night and while he slept I dreamed of him, I dreamed of him falling off of my bed, or was I dropping him, or was he in the bed and I had forgotten and I had rolled over onto him, and imagined him in the sheets or comforter, suffocated, smothered? I wake at five am and search for him, dig my hands into my husband's back; I wake my husband who was finally asleep, who still hasn't forgiven me.*

MARIGOLD (see also: Sensuous Bean, The; and Separateness): "Dr. Prince told me that he feels sorry for me," Dr. Y— told me one day. Dr. Prince, who worked in a neighboring office, had noted the many and pretty young women who came to see him. The next day, I took the train with a woman named Marigold. We volunteered together at Gilda's Club, played with little children whose parents had cancer, whose parents, like mine, may or may not die before their children understand death. On the train Marigold and I talked about our shrinks. I confessed that I had a minor crush on mine, who was on the Upper West Side. "Don't tell me it's Dr. Y—," she said. "But it is," I stuttered, as we stared at each other. We were on the 1 Train. We held the bar, my red nails touching her long thin fingers. Our faces were close;[1] it occurred to me that we could make-out without moving much at all. Marigold stared. "I'm very jealous of you," she whispered. "He used to be my doctor. I broke our contract and now he won't see me." I was drawn to something cinematic in Marigold's madness, despair. I understood why doctors were compelled by her, how she might inspire. Like Angelica Huston

---

[1] Marigold was tall, beautiful in that old money East Coast way. There was something about her, some confidence, that attracted me, despite my feelings of hopeless inferiority. It was something I've decided belongs to East Coast women but will never belong to me. A savvy. Despite her suffering, she knew how to be in the world in a way I do not. Where I am fragments, she was an entire composition.

in *Crimes and Misdemeanors,* Marigold possessed that wild, surface-level passion. "What was your contract?" "I was not allowed to have a drink. I had to stay sober to stay in therapy. One day, I was waiting for him, and I went to the bar down the block on Amsterdam. I had a drink, a few, and then showed up at his office. I was really drunk." "He kicked you out?" "Not right away. But later. He said we were through. I couldn't come back." "I'm in love with him," she told me, and her eyes looked beyond me, to a point unknown. Dr. Y— was not exactly sexy but I knew what she meant. He was seductive, spoke in low tones, looked into my eyes with intensity. He would moan occasionally, as I spoke, telling him of my day or my suffering. He was fully, physically empathic. It was like sex this way. I could reveal my secret suffering and be understood. Sitting in the adjacent leather chair I could come close to bridging the gap, the horror of separateness. He talked about his days in the army. He spoke of the "dirty" Arabs, switching into Hebrew, cursing the enemy.

MARY (see also: Ionesco, Eugene), the character in *The Bald Soprano*. I walked by the Samuel Beckett Theatre on Tenth Avenue. I once played Mary, the maid, representative of the threatening Dionysian. In the theater each night, on a stage or in a costume, I experienced, for a moment, the sense of being held.

MARRIAGE, as when my teacher and I spoke of ambivalence and relationships and I told him, "I know I will get married someday," after he'd said that I didn't want to be married, not really. It was something he could see about me, he said. That I was like him. Solitary. I insisted that he was wrong and that I saw the value in marriage, especially as one grows old. "I don't want to die alone," I told him. I was being optimistic. He scoffed. He wouldn't look at me. He made a noise before saying, "Darling, you die alone no matter what."

MASO, CAROLE, (see also: *Ava*): "We live once. And rather badly."

MCCARTHY, MARY (see also: Whitney Museum of American Art), Leaving the Paul Thek show, you run into a woman who once became famous for writing about female sexual desire; it will feel strange or wonderful or serendipitous. As a girl, this writer inspired you. You may have even moved to New York, chosen Barnard, because of her. You touch her arm. She nods, asks about your baby. You think about her sex life. You talk about her grandchildren and your grandmother and breast-feeding. "She wants to look at art," her husband will say, cutting her off, leaving you alone.

MEMORY, A high school teacher reading a poem about a married woman who wanted the gas attendant to put a hand on her breast; who wanted to grab a pretty woman; a friend burning with desire, complaining about the *normative brotherly lust* of marriage. And the way you giggled, you and your silly Catholic schoolgirl classmates, embarrassed for the teacher, wishing away her gooey lust.

MISERY (see also: Cioran, Emil; and Writing): "The literary man? An indiscreet man, who devaluates his miseries, divulges them, tells them like so many beads: immodesty—the side-show of second thoughts—is his rule; he offers himself."

THE MORGAN LIBRARY (see also: Boredom, and Beauty), where you read Charlotte Bronte's diary, written while teaching in Brussels. "So bored!" she writes. Later, Ruskin: "I feel greatly humiliated by the beauty of everything."

MOTHER(S)/MOTHERING (see also: Bliss, and Desire),

> Dearest, Yesterday I visited a friend with a new baby, a friend who told me that she does not feel as happy as she should feel. That she expected to feel sheer bliss at the arrival of her second child, but instead it has been something else, a letdown. She does not have a personality like mine, she does not tend toward darkness, and so it surprised me to hear her speak this way. But I understood her, though I cannot understand. I understand, I say.

MÜLLER, HEINER (see also: Love, and Theater): "The only thing a work of art can achieve is to create the desire for a different state of the world. And this desire is revolutionary."

MUSEUM (see also: Art, Love, and Presence),

> Yesterday I left you to see an artist. Don't laugh when I write that it felt religious—the show, my experience of the artist and her work. I watched Abramović lift her head to meet a woman's gaze. Her long hair pulled back, a long red dress. I watched a woman hold her gaze, tears in the artist's eyes. This happened over and over again. A long moment passed. She returned.

MUSICIAN (see also: Body, and Healing), You observe a friend, a musician, who is completely and utterly in his body. When he speaks, his chest rises and falls, his eyes focus, his laugh is a thing separate from himself. The dream: to be in the world, to be in your body.

NARDIL (see also: M.A.O.I., and Regret), as when you run into a woman doctor who saved your life once. Her face now recalls your mother's frozen beauty. *Have you injected botulism into your face?* She advises you to have another child. You have been too ambivalent; your husband has not wanted another child; you are too selfish, too *something*. "If it were to happen," you explain—as if you need validation for your life choices—"it would have been just after Magoo was born," while you were still lost, contained and within the ecstasy of maternity: bloated, a maternal thing, your body not your own. The woman offers her "clinical bias" against only children: "It is a difficult life, a heavy burden."

NEGATION (see also: Dybek, Stuart), "Let us explore the literature of negation. Of absence," you declare. Literary notions too sexy for a classroom, which is where you come upon most sexy notions. You read from Dybek's story: "I was the DH Lawrence of not doing it." We blush.

NEWS (see also: Statistics), A *headline* hovers over your in-box that morning: "MOST CHILDREN GET OVER THE SUDDEN DEATH OF A PARENT." The subtitle: *10% at risk for severe depression.*

NEW YORK TIMES, THE (see also: Exceptions, and Marriage), B— was "going through a divorce"—a concept which seemed foreign, far away, dirty. His wife was 35 when they married. "We *looked good on paper*," he told you. Which also felt foreign. The way New Yorkers care about paper. Marriage and 35 and divorce were all very far away. You find the announcement in the online archive. It doesn't look good online.

NEW YORK CITY (see also: Bad Relationships)—if New York was the site of deepest despair, it also offered a life imbued with immense meaning.[1] Perhaps education is made more meaningful to one in a state of lethal

---

[1] As Georgia O'Keeffe wrote in 1976: "In 1925 while living in New York City, I began talking about trying to paint New York.

despair, of insatiable need? I looked to books, to the city[2] itself, for nothing less than instruction on how to live.

NIN, ANAÏS, (see also: Human, and Maternity), A critic notes Nin's "chilling inhumanity." He describes this scene: Nin takes pills, which don't work, to induce an abortion; at six months she gives birth to a stillborn baby girl. "These legs I opened to joy, this honey that flowed out in the joy—now these legs are twisted in pain and the honey flows with the blood. The same pose and the same wetness of passion but this is dying and not loving." In 1978 Cacherel released a perfume called Anaïs Anaïs,[3] which a teenage girl receives for her

---

Of course, I was told that it was an impossible idea—even the men hadn't done too well with it. From my teens on I had been told that I had crazy notions so I was accustomed to disagreement and went on with my idea of painting New York. One can't paint New York as it is, but rather as it is felt."

[2] Exiting the subway at 77th, I see Mary, who wrote a song for me when I lived at 53rd and 9th. At that time she was 37, which seemed tragically old. I had been in love with the actor who didn't love me and since Mary did love me, or thought she did, we would go into the bedroom, close the door, and she'd go down on me. My roommate would sit outside, waiting for us.

[3]   A perfume that has nothing to do with freedom. Which was perhaps connected to desire by the promise that a man would love you

14th birthday. She smells the sweet floral scents, notes the shape of the bottle, flowers carved out of thick glass. She knows nothing of Nin's radical manifesto, or her belief in personal freedom or transformative, transcendent love. She thumbtacks index cards with Nin's words all over the bedroom wall: "Life shrinks or expands in proportion to one's courage," and "Life is truly known only to those who suffer, lose, endure adversity and stumble from defeat to defeat." *Knowledge is constructed.*

---

desire you via this perfume which of course is a lie. I have most desired dark and disturbing smells of my lover, the smells that have to do with sweat and fluids and carnality. These smells have always been more erotic than a toxic synthetic perfume or cologne would ever be. All of this is to say, simply, I love the smell of you.

OBLIVION (see also: Forty), Our teacher assigned us an essay by the poet Donald Justice, about what happens to writers when they reach a certain age. Justice writes of turning to art as spiritual vocation[1] that occurs usually when one is adolescent, a dedication akin to that of religious sects. Members spot it in each other; the elder can see it in the younger. The shining. A sensitivity. Justice writes of a crisis that occurs later, when the pursuit of the ideal proves elusive. This is perhaps the argument of Fitzgerald in *The Crack-Up*. The rest of the

---

[1] Some of us found the poet's characterization of the solitary artist excessively romantic. It is romantic, but for others, this is where we live. This excess. Art saves us—provides hope. The governor speaks of the importance of art, which strengthens the soul, he says. Or destroys/confronts/conquers the soul.

essay is an examination of the careers of three obscure poets who came to crisis mid-career. Each eventually committed suicide, which Justice reads as a result of this crisis. He seems to read the pursuit of artistic vocation as the promise of oblivion. I do not object to that part of the argument—our teacher's death would be linked to a crisis in his artistic life. I read it in his last, unfinished book, a book saturated with crisis, as Duras' late books are saturated with alcoholism, saturated in a way that does not satisfy, only opens a space, compels a reader toward that void. But there is a truth in saturation, in excess.[2]

---

[2] —but I want to believe that it is possible to live beyond forty, to live with a ravaged, ruined face to live within the totality of fear and despair. I once believed that having gone mad as a young woman would protect me from the inevitable. Now I know that was naive—

PARENTING, A woman tells her nine-year-old daughter, who is eating chips: "A moment on your lips, a lifetime on your hips!" A neighbor calls out to his three-year-old: "Get up! You are okay! You are okay! High five! High five!"

PASSIVE INTENTIONALITY, a friend calls it, warning you.

PAPER (see also: Heartbreak), "He was important. I was 26; he was 46. Now he is my Facebook friend. I occasionally see his updates, noting his television appearances, airline commercials. It had to do with timing. I fell out of love. But when it began he did not love me enough. This is how it felt to me. That he would not love me enough and perhaps that was where it was meant to stay—me wanting more, wanting him to love me more; him just out of reach. He was going through a divorce—a concept that seemed foreign, far away and dirty. His wife was 35 when they married. 'We looked good on paper,' he told me. Which also felt foreign. How New Yorkers care about paper. Marriage and 35 and divorce were all very far away. I read the announcement in the *Times* archive."

PATHOS (see also: Religion),

> Dearest, I think we are lovely. I think we are searching, blind, groping in the dark. I went to church yesterday, where I haven't been in years. The priest quoted Keats. He noted that we are all Zaccheaus—but I feared the inherent antisemitism. I want things to be different. I want to believe in God. I want to believe in something.

PERRY STREET (see also: *Hamlet*), where privileged students sit together in a Czech cafe, take pictures of one another which they instantly post on the internet after discussing who *to follow or not to follow*; which photo app is *most* or *least* flattering. "You can't just tag people!" one tells another. "I don't know how to do hashtags!" "I don't believe you!"

PETE'S CANDY STORE, where you listen to a poet. "We have an open relationship," the man explains. He sleeps with anyone. The woman leans toward you, says hello. You think of kissing her lips and together, or so it seems, the two of you imagine this kiss, there in greeting. You are the older woman in this scenario. "How old are you?" she asks. 37. "I'm 27," she says. It feels significant. "We are sisters," she whispers. You try to remember being 27 but only vaguely do so—you recall something of the way you felt your life must begin or you would die of it. Or that life was not what you supposed it would be, which was still surprising at 27. "Brooklyn is death for writers." "I understand," you say. "I chose Normal over Brooklyn." She laughs. "And that has made all the difference." Behind you women are speaking loudly.[1] The younger woman returns to your face, the incipient kiss, to tell the story of her mother. "She wanted to kill me when I was a baby. She wanted to put me in the dryer." "On the dryer?" you suggest. You have heard of this, a soothing strategy. "On the dryer!" you repeat, nodding, a bit hysterical. "No. *In* the dryer." "I haven't heard that one," you shrug. And then,

---

[1] "I believe that all males under 35 should not be allowed to speak more than once each workshop."

"Or that any male under 35 must write his comments in one sentence on a one inch space and that's it."

"I like your mother." "Because she almost killed me?"
"That's not what I meant," you say, too late.

PHAEDRA (see also: Lacan, Poetry, and Racine), In *Coeur de
Lion*, Ariana Reines writes "I love when Racine makes
Phaedra say I LOVE instead Of I LOVE YOU. She
was Not too proud." Simone Weil calls Phaedra's love
impure. That in Phaedra's case, *the passion of love goes
as far as vegetative energy*. Says Sontag: "The obscene,
that is to say, the extremity of erotic experience, is the
root of vital energies. Human beings live only through
excess."

PHILOSOPHY, Your analyst will say "Your marriage is
not working because you are depressed," and you will
agree; your friend will say "You are depressed because
your marriage is not working," and you will agree.

PLATH, SYLVIA, assessed this way: "Her self-aggran-
dizing gestures invite attention, and yet we are to be
ashamed of ourselves if we accept the invitation."

PLEASURE (see also: Eggs, and Writing), Occasionally x is
not pleasurable and yet we pursue it. We need it, re-
gardless. Even when it's not. When it's something
else, something apart from pleasure. When I am not

writing, everything inside of me that needs to be written revolts. I might scream, pass out—[2]

POPO MARTIN, a character in Nicky Silver's play *Fat Men in Skirts* announces, "I'm the most popular girl in the mental hospital!" She calls her diagnosis "Marnie's disease": "You know, like Tippie Hendren in that movie." She is the kind of mental patient who needs the romance or the humor because the alternative—that we'd failed, that we were fuck-ups, losers, time-wasters—is more difficult to stomach. We all needed to be reminded that Allen Ginsberg and Marilyn Monroe and James Taylor and Sylvia Plath had been mental patients. Otherwise, well, we might have to face the thought that our lives meant nothing—which was surely something we suspected, sitting as we did in the common room with other chemically-induced stoics, drooling or sleeping or watching television footage of OJ's white SUV being chased by the Los Angeles police department.

---

[2] This is why I was admitted to a hospital once, long ago. A suffocating pain on my chest. This thing. Nerves, they would say, as if that meant anything. I would think of Blanche DuBois when they said this, think of her delicate constitution, her desire for Stanley. It would never be enough: refinement, sensitivity. There was no room in this American life.

PROFESSOR (see also: Cocoa, and Pedagogy), One day I gain the courage to go to his office hours to discuss Beckett but really to see if he could tell me how I might continue to live and in the midst of that conversation, in an offhanded way, he sighed, saying: "That's the thing about life: you can't get out of it alive."

PSYCHOSIS, as when the man in boots refers to his Super Ego. You feel female around him, linked to the Dionysian; that something in you promises destruction. That you were made to be repressed. Women are linked to the pleasure-seeking Id. What Aase Berg calls the "positive psychosis" of mothering. What Sophie Freud called passion. A sense of invincibility. A madness. You understand sublimation and yet you are trying to say something about this certain psychosis. This is the horror of the world. "What are your parenting plans?" he asks and you answer incorrectly. He laughs at your ambivalence.

PUNISHMENT, A friend is overwhelmed by her life, which involves working toward tenure, delivering papers on micro-finance, caring for babies. We speak of raising children into moral beings; how to avoid punishment & reward, *conditional* parenting. She reads

Alfie Kohn, Adele Faber, Dr. Sears. Her mother tells us that these ideas are *retarded,* declares: "They have to learn table manners!"

PREEXISTING FORMS (see also: Bidart, Frank), as in, "We fill pre-existing forms and when we fill them change them and are changed." It will occur to you: you are the one now, the wise one, the one to tell the young girl, with an arm firmly extended, "I am worried about you."

QUERY (see also: Hysteria)

RANKINE, CLAUDIA (see also: Loneliness), On the plane home from New York, you read *Don't Let Me Be Lonely*. "Thinking as if trying to weep." This is you. Always *thinking as if trying to weep*. A colleague lends it to you, cannot stop telling you about this book, and yes, you say, you'll read it. You have been needing this book for years—and she knew: "Define loneliness?/ Yes. / It's what we can't do for each other. / What do we mean to each other? / What does a life mean? / Why are we here if not for each other?" You sink into your seat and the man next to you takes up more than his share of space. His broad body leaks into the space of your seat and you want to reject the intrusive body in a way that is neither polite nor civil. Instead it seeps into you and you ache until he asks you about your book; "What do you write?" "I am writing a book about the liver," you say plagiarizing the narrator of Rankine's book. You hope this will encourage him to move his arm that is nearly in your lap. You will come to understand this as a feminist issue. Now his hand is on your thigh; instead of telling him to move his hand, you decide to propose a conference paper on this: *The Dynamics of Gendered Bodies. Bodies in Space. Spatial Planes and Bodies.* Soon you forget your body. You look out the window, wait for New York to be a place you can leave— it refuses—a place you reject, which you can't. Unlike the man, the arm of the man, the hand of the man. You long to leave the liminal state where you look to the city as an opening, where you look to your life as a creation.

REAL, THE (see also: Crazy), Something else the man in boots has admired, reading you: he wants to understand how you managed to create a "crazy sounding" voice without "really" sounding crazy.

REALITY, as when the same man speaks of the life that is real and the life that is unreal. As when you ask: "How can one tell the difference?" (As when a student wears a t-shirt that declares: *Cute But Psycho*.) Or the way you forget that his interest in you is wholly professional, that he wants something. You forget and you feel a connection, to the promise of his body—black denim jacket, clumsy Timberland boots— across from your own, which is hysterical and problematic, an insoluble problem. You stand next to him. He will bring you water, Dixie cups' full, over and over again. You are so thirsty.

REBIRTH, (see also: Ginsberg, Allen) Perhaps Ginsberg, too, saw the ward as a place for those who sought spiritual transcendence, even while the place itself reduced that search. Still, it was a place, an alternative. A place to find fellows: Carl Solomon. Chuck. Q—.

RECOGNITION (see also: Bowles, Jane), on meeting Paul Bowles: "The first time I saw him I said to a friend, he's my enemy."

REDUX (see also: Narcissism), A student will say, "I hate language." "I used to be that way," you'll tell him.

REINES, ARIANA, (see also: Phaedra) "Maybe long ago things were too / Too solid, and now we live in an ether / Of ex-sentiments, impossible / To make sense of except for wet / Panties, something that even / In hindsight might never / Consolidate into a real emotion."

REHEARSAL (see also: Love), when a director channels Van Gogh: "There is nothing more truly artistic than to love another person."

RELIGION (see also: Beckett, Samuel; Death; Desire; God; Godot; and Memory):

DIDI: Do you believe in the life to come?

GOGO: Mine was always that.

RENDEZVOUS, as when the man in boots suggests a meeting. Life opens into possibility. He will write: *coffee/tea/danish*? It will turn you on. You will wonder about yourself. But not so much as to stop you from replying, and too quickly: *Yes*.

REVELATION (see also: Anecdote, Discourse, and Mothering), A friend describes her mother-in-law: "normalizing."

ROMANCE (see also: Victim), I read *Justine* and *The Golden Notebook* and *Wuthering Heights*, the theory of Julia Kristeva and Judith Butler. Each is glorified female masochism that simultaneously rejects the narrative. I wrote papers on Kathy Acker. Here is what you might not know: it was satisfying. To be sick, to be mad. That is the dirty little secret that is not a secret, no. Sometimes, I miss it. As Sontag wrote in her journal: "My dream of madness: being no longer capable of the effort to make contact."

SACRAMENTS (see also: Thek, Paul), in which Thek writes, "to feel okay in spite of it all / to feel good knowing all the worst."

SAD, or you might feel alive again, connected again to something that has been lost. You might imagine accessing the infinite through the man in boots, through *this*—which is all you've ever wanted.

SANITY (see also: Truth), Susan Sontag writes that of course she comes down on the side of sanity that of course no one would wish for his/her child to live as Simone Weil and yet everyone reads Simone Weil, searching for the truth that they know she possessed. Sontag begins in a flurry, stating that Weil's truth was necessary for this age that it was the hysteric voice that we needed a truth to contrast with the other problematic voices and yet what we also know was that it was not true. In conclusion she states that she believes in the truth of sanity, but she will not say that the voice of insanity is untrue.

SCHWARTZ, DELMORE (see also: Prophecy, Husband), "All poet's wives / have ruined lives."

SCREWTAPE LETTERS, THE (see also: Memory), The first time, I roomed with a woman who was reading C.S. Lewis. She didn't have anything else with her in that room. She gently encouraged me to read this book. One example of the humanity one encounters in the midst of institutionalized suffering.

SELF, (see also: Iveković, Sanja; MOMA; and Meaning), as when you stand beside the man in boots, read aloud: "The fictive aspects of public and private narratives. The intersection of history with the private self. Makeup does a lot."

SELF-PORTRAIT WITH SKULL (see also: Teaching, and Violence) as when you stand in front of a video of Marina Abramović, who beats herself in the gut, a skull in her hands, over and over again. Hair in her face, her large breasts exposed. After some time, you feel the beating in your own gut and brain[1] and it feels right. When you walk back out into the street the fog is thick and low. A young boy tells you that he feels depression the way Plath describes it in "Lady Lazarus": his mind skews, he sees the world differently, it feels genocidal. "Thank you for telling me," you say. "I'll see you next week," you add, because you worry. You make him promise. You pretend to be a teacher but mostly you are ALL FEELING ALL THE TIME and so fucked up by it, a disintegrated dislocated self.

SEARCHING (see also: Desire), as when you tell a friend: "What I mean is that there is nothing so attractive to me as someone who is searching, has sought. Someone lost, a certain registered suffering."

SEDUCTION, as when the man in boots tells you that he's read your book. Poetry: *academic, obscure, abstruse* the critics describe it. No one reads your book, but he will read it: thoughtfully, carefully.

SENSUOUS BEAN, THE (see also: Memory), which was the name of the coffee shop I passed each time I walked

---

[1] Make "the head throb heartlike"—

from the subway at 72nd to Dr. Y—'s office. One day I wore a purple felt mini-skirt that zipped up the back. Black tights. Doc Martens. My memory is lit up with the feel of that purple skirt, the look of it: *a young woman who wants to be the object of the gaze and is disgusted by the gaze.* Dr. Y— greeted me with a warm smile. His charisma. Something inside of me, that bone below my stomach. He looked at me, said how much he liked it. "My skirt?" I asked. He shook his head. "Your whole gestalt."[2]

SHRINK (see also: Belief), as when you tell the specialist: "I don't know what *mentally ill* means. Does it mean that I find this world disgusting? Does it mean that I vomit? Does it mean that, like Fanny Howe, I believe that art must show that life is worth living by showing that it isn't?"

SICK (see also: Madness), Years later, Q— ends up in a hospital in NYC. This was in the nineties. He is still in

---

[2] I didn't know I had a gestalt, though I did, and this word became as significant to the memory as did the feel of my hips in that purple skirt. Also, the feeling when I left his office, that ache. There was nothing that could fill it. Nothing. In his office, on occasion, I felt this: *alive*.

a hospital. Back home, I run into his father who tells me how "sick" poor Q— remains.

SILENCE (see also: Barthes, Roland; and Teaching), as when a colleague writes on the whiteboard to his students: *Go to where the silence is and say something.* Or when you enter the classroom after him, leave his line, but add another: *All Identities are Fictions.*

SONTAG, SUSAN (see also: Inspiration, Skunks, and Truth): "Art must mount a full-scale attack on language itself, by means of language and its surrogates, on behalf of the standard of silence."

SOUP (see also: Duras, Marguerite): "You can want to do nothing and then decide instead to do this: make leek broth. Between the will to do something and the will to do nothing is a thin, unchanging line: suicide."

SOUTHWEST AIRLINES, Waiting for your flight, you see a commercial for an airlines featuring B—, an actor, a man you loved. Over the phone, you told him about the roaches in your apartment and he told you it was time to come back to New York. You told him he didn't understand, that you aren't coming back. Later you had phone sex.

STEIG, WILLIAM (see also: Mothers, and Walls), You read William Steig books to Magoo; you try to skip lines. He catches you. "No. Read this page, Mama." You are caught, a fraud, skipping through *Doctor De Soto*. "You don't read very well Mama." He sleeps, you grade student essays so terrible you don't know where to begin; you stop yourself from scribbling *THIS SUCKS* in bright red Sharpie across a title page you sign with a smiley face: *Sincerely, Yr Instructor*. You recall your teacher, throwing a student essay across his living room, the essay hitting the wall. Your satisfaction as he told you this story.

SUICIDE (see also: Soup), as when a friend writes to tell you that he has seventeen papers left to grade, and this is making him suicidal. *Ridiculous but true*, he writes. *I get it*, you write back. "Duras once linked the making of leek soup to suicide," you explain. Later you read something the writer Blake Butler has written on the Internet about your teacher. Blake didn't know him, but has long adored his work. He "gave up," Blake wrote. *He did give up*, you think. *Which is all I've ever wanted to do.* Blake went on, "For the past ten years, I have thought about him almost every day." In this, he acknowledges our cultural moment: the obsession that drove this essay, that drives the biographer, the listserv, the fan club, the posting of your now-dead teacher's autopsy report online[3].

---

[3] —*as unseemly as your death was, gruesome as it was, we were all thinking about you and your belt and I'm not supposed to talk about it for days and nights though it was none of our business and you were allowed. Though we have to allow it of you, though we revere you for it now, though you make us sick and we love you now with an intensity that embarrasses us. The intensity we reserve for the dead, for our love of the dead. You were beautiful we realize now and it sickens us. That we'd forgotten or hadn't noticed.*

TEACHING (see also: Days, and Containment)—I head downtown, after putting my body in a skirt so that I might be contained to teach to contain myself to fill my life with structure and busyness so that I might be unlike the fever of my summer contained against the pull towards madness so that I might be contained in structure so that I might ignore the ways that I feel myself—trying to protect myself from loneliness, longing, boredom—what you once thought adulthood itself would protect against a marriage meant to shield you—the institution of marriage—you allowed yourself to be institutionalized again—

TEETH (see also: M.A.O.I., and Nardil), "One side effect is to reduce saliva, leading to dry mouth," a dental student explains. "Anti-depressants in general, but M.A.O.I.s in particular, damage teeth." He suggests extracting one tooth.[1]

TEXAS (see also: Horror)

THEATER (see also: Containment, Madwomen, and Memory),

> My dearest, these women will always be with me. I don't know where they are, if they are alive or dead. But they often appear to me, and in the most unexpected moments. I used to walk by Meredith's room and catch her arranging her many tiny glass figurines on the shelves of her room. She would spend hours arranging and, because our rooms didn't have doors, I often watched her. No one was allowed to have glass, but for Meredith an exception was made. She needed the figurines, needed to arrange, needed to be contained. The allusion to Tennessee Williams was so heavy, so obvious, that no one spoke of it. Maybe Dr. Y— spoke of it, in one of his lectures to medical students. It was the kind of detail he savored.

---

[1] This was just after I'd left New York. I didn't have health insurance. Somehow the extraction of that tooth came to represent an unparalleled low point; a psychic/spiritual nadir.

THEK, PAUL (See also: McCarthy, Mary; Roman Catholicism; and Whitney Museum of American Art), The writer's husband interrupts, "Save it for the book, Erica," he urges. I want him to go away. "She's trying to look at art," he tells her, though what I wish is to continue our conversation. Instead I read of Paul Thek: "He was not afraid to use HOT content, at a time when artists were so focused on form."

THIRTIES (see also: Reines, Ariana; Uncensored; and Writing)

TIME, as when you tell him you have plenty. Which you have not told anyone in years. Or, much later, the thought that you don't believe in such a thing, that it may not exist.[2]

---

[2] Dear X, Do you remember when I was 20 and you were 30 and now I am old and you are older and yet we were there yesterday facing a New York life beside each other. Ours lives mattered, yes? I see that now. Yesterday I thought of you, wanted to see you to touch you after I rode the train with the young Barnard girls beside me. I wanted to tell you that it was there in front of me the truth that time does not exist—just yesterday I had her milky skin just yesterday I stood on this train with the others feeling so disconnected and convinced they were all so much much more well-adjusted than I or me or I. Which they were, you have to admit, I did have a point now didn't I? And now, how will I fit into my bourgeois life?

TIMING, where, as with all else, it will return.

TRAFFIC, "I'll send you the link to click and read—will you, so you can build her traffic?" "I'll click but I won't read." "Yeah." "I'll click." "You don't have to read."

TRAGEDY (see also: Good People), as when you tell him that you are happy that the two of you are going to be friends.

TRANSMISSION (see also: Emptiness), I walk to the train. The sun begins to set. I don't want to force anyone to be in a room with me. I don't want them to read because they have to. I see how textbooks and a syllabus ruin art. It must be outside of control. Even though much came to me in a classroom, within the academy, I long for something wild.

TRIANGULATION (see also: Marriage, and Sestina), On Day Ten, the man will tell you that he is writing a sestina for a woman. You will tell him that your husband writes sestinas. Would he like to read your husband's sestinas? You will know that it is inappropriate to mention your husband's talent with the sestina. But then you will remember: he is not your boyfriend. He is married. You were just trying to be a grownup, you will say, apologizing. You tell him that you don't know the etiquette. "Is there etiquette?" you ask. He will say "Yes." The first piece of etiquette, he explains, is that you don't mention your husband.

UNRELENTING, or the consistency, the persistence of the city wearies me. That one might leave for ten, fifteen years, only to return and find it all again. Also, the simplicity of it: a city rendering one insane. You tell the man about a movie you've seen where one actor describes to another the way he thinks of New York as a new kind of insane asylum, where the inmates police themselves through smug self-satisfaction.

VICTIM (see also: Erotically Attached, Intentional Passivity, and Status),

> Dearest, I lived there for two or maybe it was three—
> see I can't remember, I was so drugged—back in the
> 90s with women who were passive, masochistic, enam-
> ored of their victim status. There were dancers/actors/
> performers among us. Of course. Looking to the great
> white male medical establishment for solace and cure.
> Nurturing your sickness with a desire to be held, to be
> loved, to be cured. To be fucked. The implied desire for
> obliteration, annihilation. I wonder about us, now that
> I am old. I am trying to write about this. I have long
> been trying to write about this. I have written this fifty
> different ways, there are multiple versions, ways I could
> tell you this story, but lately I think the way is through
> the woman herself.

VOLVO (see also: Our Teacher), *Do you remember how I came alive in the back of your Volvo the constraints of the space allowing freedom how I shrieked and wept the seat belt latch sharp in my left buttock you licking my clit the anticipation of a car slowing down. Let's christen it you said. I flinched. And you sighed and I said fine then okay show me and there we were before I knew what or how first my face on the floor next your mouth on my clit the sharp latch again you are so wet you said and when I came you said again come again and I came again. This is how you christen it? I said my leg over your shoulder now and Yes this is how you said Yes my hands in your hair wanting to something but your face gone now yes this is Christ.*

WARD SIX (see also: Memory, and Theater), Over tapioca pudding, an oboist discovers that you attend Barnard. "But that's a school for good Jewish girls," he wonders aloud. "I am hoping to be a New York Jewish intellectual," you say.

WEIL, SIMONE (see also: Desire, and Emptiness), "To see each human being (an image of oneself) as a prison in which a prisoner dwells, surrounded by the whole universe."

WIFE, to whom, one day, the man in boots will compare you. It isn't a compliment.

WISHES (see also: Desire, Life, Love, and Teaching), And toward the luxurious quotidian: I wish for one or two more students like the one who shook my hand and said "It's been a pleasure," or the one who said "Thank you for the semester," as if it were a gift (it was) or the one who asked me to watch his favorite movie and then whispered, "And email me after you do." *A Single Man*. A sad movie, from a Christopher Isherwood novel I haven't read. A day in the life of a grieving man. I email the student but I don't tell him that I understand that grief, how perception alters, shifts, what it is to be undone by grief, the effort that must go into daily life. I tell him that I was moved by the highly stylized, melancholy movie. I tell him I liked especially when the single man tells a student: the only thing that's made the whole thing worthwhile has been those few times when I've been able to really truly connect with another human being.

WOOLF, VIRGINIA (see also: Cabbages; and *Waves, The*): "Something now leaves me; something goes from me to meet that figure who is coming, and assures me that I know him before I see who it is. How curiously one is changed by the addition, even at a distance, of a friend. How useful an office one's friends perform when they recall us. Yet how painful to be recalled, to be mitigated, to have one's self adulterated, mixed up, become part of another."

WORKSHOP (see also: *Feminaissance*), as when a student tells another: "The problem with this essay is that it's too emotional."

WRITING (see also: Cixous, Hélène): "To my sincere surprise, which is only the product of a form of blindness, I realized in time that the writers I love above all are of the dying-clairvoyant kind."

X/XING, (see also: X Marks the Spot, X-Rated, and X'ed Out), which might refer to sex, or to love, or to you. "The thing is: I really need you with me in this story."

ACKNOWLEDGMENTS

Thank you to the editors who previously published selections from this Index in the *Iowa Review* and *Hobart*.

Endless thanks to Amanda Goldblatt and Anne Yoder.

This book would not exist if it weren't for the intellectual, spiritual and artistic guidance of these beautiful people: Daniel Borzutzky, Lorenzo Borzutzky, Erin Oleskey, Kate Zambreno, Danielle Dutton, Martin Riker, Amina Cain, Paul Rusconi, David Adjmi, Nathan Heiges, Erin Teegarden, Gregory Howard, Kathleen Odell, Mark Booth, and Curtis White.

Other writers and texts I've copied, (mis)quoted, refor-
mulated, or otherwise invoked in the creation of this
book: Judith Butler in "Giving an Account of Oneself"; Virginia Woolf in *Mrs. Dalloway*; Kate Zambreno in *Heroines* and on her blog *Frances Farmer is My
Sister* (as Kate is mine); Phillip Larkin in *Church Go-
ing*; E. M. Cioran in "Some Blind Alleys"; Susan Sontag in *Reborn* and various essays; Samuel Beckett in
Waiting for Godot, Eugene Ionesco in *Man With Bags*,
Tony Kushner, Stuart Davis, Tennessee Williams in
Streetcar Named Desire; Kathy Acker in *In Memoriam
to Identity*, Eileen Myles in an interview with Jackie
Wang; Paul Thek's *Meat Pieces*, Marguerite Duras in
Writing and *Hiroshima, Mon Amour*; Edna St. Vincent
Millay in her poems; Maggie Nelson in *Bluets*, Simone
Weil in *Gravity and Grace*; Annie Ernaux in *The Pos-
session*; Chris Kraus and Dodie Bellamy in *Feminais-
sance*, Elizabeth Hardwick in *Seduction and Betrayal*
and *Sleepless Nights*; Carole Maso in *Ava* and *Break
Every Rule*; David Foster Wallace in *Infinite Jest*; Noah
Baumbach's *Greenberg*; Jean Rhys in *Good Morning,
Midnight*; Allan Ginsberg in *Howl*; Oscar Wilde;
Elizabeth Bishop in "One Art"; Chris Kraus in *I Love
Dick*; Daphne Merkin in "The Black Season"; Ariana

Reines in *Coeur de Lion* and *The Cow*; Racine in *Phaedra*; Nicky Silver in *Fat Men in Skirts*; Clarice Lispector in *Soulstorm*; Sanja Iveković in *Double Life*; Anne Carson in an interview with Dinitia Smith; Heiner Müller; Marina Abramović in *The Artist is Present* and *Self-Portrait with Skull*; Stuart Dybek in "We Didn't"; Georgia O'Keeffe in *Georgia O'Keeffe*; Donald Justice in "Oblivion"; F. Scott Fitzgerald in "The Crack-Up"; Frank Bidart in *Desire*; Claudia Rankine in *Don't Let Me Be Lonely*; Blake Butler on Facebook; Hélène Cixous in *Three Steps on the Ladder of Writing*; Wallace Shawn in *My Dinner With Andre*; *The Seminar of Jacques Lacan*, Mary Gordon in "Flannery's Kiss."

This book is for Danny.